my itty-bitty bio

P.K. Subban

CHERRY LAKE PRESS

Published in the United States of America by Cherry Lake Publishing
Ann Arbor, Michigan
www.cherrylakepublishing.com

Reading Adviser: Marla Conn, MS, Ed., Literacy specialist, Read-Ability, Inc.
Book Designer: Jennifer Wahl
Illustrator: Jeff Bane

Photo Credits: © Derek Sutton/Shutterstock, 5; © DardaInna/Shutterstock, 7; © Richard Bartlaga/Flickr, 9; © Kristina Servant/Flickr, 11, 22; © Brian Cassella/Chicago Tribune/MCT/Alamy Live News, 13, 23; © Walt Disney Television/Flickr, 15 © meunierd/Shutterstock, 17; © Lucky Business/Shutterstock, 19; © DFree/Shutterstock, 21; Cover, 1, 6, 10, 14, Jeff Bane; Various frames throughout, © Shutterstock images

Cherry Lake Press is an imprint of Cherry Lake Publishing Group.

Library of Congress Cataloging-in-Publication Data

Names: Pincus, Meeg, author. | Bane, Jeff, 1957- illustrator.
Title: P.K. Subban / Meeg Pincus ; illustrated by Jeff Bane.
Description: Ann Arbor, Michigan : Cherry Lake Publishing, 2021. | Series: My itty-bitty bio | Includes index. | Audience: Grades K-1
Identifiers: LCCN 2020005688 (print) | LCCN 2020005689 (ebook) | ISBN 9781534168428 (hardcover) | ISBN 9781534170100 (paperback) | ISBN 9781534171947 (pdf) | ISBN 9781534173781 (ebook)
Subjects: LCSH: Subban, P. K., 1989---Juvenile literature. | Hockey players--Canada--Biography--Juvenile literature.
Classification: LCC GV848.5.S84 P56 2021 (print) | LCC GV848.5.S84 (ebook) | DDC 796.962092/271--dc23
LC record available at https://lccn.loc.gov/2020005688
LC ebook record available at https://lccn.loc.gov/2020005689

Printed in the United States of America
Corporate Graphics

table of contents

My Story 4

Timeline 22

Glossary 24

Index 24

About the author: Meeg Pincus has been a writer, editor, and educator for 25 years. She loves to write inspiring stories for kids about people, animals, and our planet. She lives near San Diego, California, where she enjoys the beach, reading, singing, and her family.

About the illustrator: Jeff Bane and his two business partners own a studio along the American River in Folsom, California, home of the 1849 Gold Rush. When Jeff's not sketching or illustrating for clients, he's either swimming or kayaking in the river to relax.

my story

I was born in Toronto, Canada. It was 1989.

I have two brothers and two sisters.

I started playing on a hockey team at 3 years old. Some people were mean to me because I am black. My parents taught me to be **confident**.

What makes you confident?

I dreamed of playing **professional** hockey like Jean Béliveau. He was a famous Canadian player. He was my **role model**. I wanted to help others like he did.

How can you help others?

I became a professional hockey player at age 20. I won awards and became an **all-star**.

76
CCM

I played in the **Olympics** for Canada. My team won the gold medal.

SOCHI 2014

I love to **design** clothes. I have a fashion company.

Capital
ESPYS
Capital One
Capita
ESPYS
ESPYS
Capital One

I also love to help others. I **donate** money to those in need. I visit kids at a children's hospital.

How do you help?

I helped a young black hockey player. He was **bullied**. I want hockey to be friendly for all.

I am a hockey star. I am a fashion designer. I love helping others. I want kids to go after their dreams.

What would you like to ask me?

timeline

2009

1980

Born 1989

2014

2080

glossary & index

glossary

all-star (AWL STAHR) chosen as one of the best players in a sport

bullied (BUL-eed) frightened or picked on by people

confident (KAHN-fih-duhnt) having a strong belief in your own abilities

design (dih-ZINE) to draw a plan for something that can be made

donate (DOH-nate) to give something to a charity or cause

Olympics (uh-LIM-piks) the summer and winter contests for athletes from all over the world

professional (pruh-FESH-uh-nuhl) making money for working hard at something others do for fun

role model (ROHL MAH-duhl) a person whose behavior is imitated by others

index

Canada, 4, 12
confident, 6
donate, 16
fashion, 14, 20
help, 8, 9, 16, 17, 18, 20
hockey, 6, 8, 10, 18, 20
kids, 16, 20
Olympics, 12
professional, 8, 10